CHEWING GUM

Mansour Bushnaf is a playwright, novelist and essayist, born in Libya, 1954. He was imprisoned for ten years in the early 1970s because of his political activism and critical writings and is renowned for his award-winning satirical plays. Chewing Gum is his first novel. He lives and works in Tripoli.

Published by DARF Publishers 2014

Copyright © Mansour Bushnaf

Translated by Mona Zaki

Cover Design by Luke Pajak

**First published in Great Britain in 2014
by DARF Publishers LTD**

277 West End Lane,London, NW6 1QS

www.darfpublishers.co.uk

ISBN No. 9781850772729

Printed and bound in Turkey

Typeset by Corporate Translations Limited - UK

www.corporatetranslations.co.uk

CHEWING GUM

by

Mansour Bushnaf

DARF PUBLISHERS
LONDON

The Beginning to Our Story

Our hero looked on as our heroine walked away in the rain, wrapped in her black coat and red shawl. Ten years went by before he was able to whisper into her ear again, ten years during which he remained standing in the exact spot where she had left him in the park, enduring his terrible suffering. Days went by, then months, and years. He waited in the rain while she walked on, hoping she would stop, turn and run back. Her red shawl fluttered gently as she headed towards the sunset, revealing her black shoulder-length hair.

At first, passersby gazed at him with consternation and lovers were startled to discover him rooted a few feet away from them. However, in time he became part of the park, indistinguishable from the tree that shaded him all those years. Children played, lovers whispered, drug dealers shook hands, prostitutes made their rounds, conspiracies were hatched, assassinations, kidnappings and rapes were carried out not far from where he stood. Yet he was conscious of nothing except her retreating, shrouded in a black coat and red shawl. His hair grew, as did his beard. His clothes became tattered, his family and friends abandoned him and the city lost track of him. He became a forgotten feature of a neglected park.

Meanwhile, Libya fell into the grip of chewing gum mania. In pursuit of this latest craze, citizens applied for passports, purchased dollars on the black market and queued up in front of airline offices, desperate to travel overseas so as to bring back the precious commodity. Gum became the rage almost overnight. Mothers listed it in their daughters' dowries and a class of smugglers mushroomed to meet the increasing demand. Such illicit activity was necessary, for commerce was deemed an illegal act, akin to smuggling, and punishable by law. In the local market, currencies rose and fell against the stable value of the gum, whose traders elevated its worth to the status of a bond. Secret study groups conducted passionate debates on the craze, its profitability, and its physical benefits. To counter this, television programmes, newspapers and even government loudspeakers tirelessly proclaimed that gum, like shampoo, was an imperialist ploy designed to destabilize the national economy, all of which fell on deaf ears.

Chewing gum acquired a philosophical dimension with the return of a professor from France, who had obtained a PhD there with a thesis on Sartre. While in France, this man had discovered a startling similarity he shared with the Gallic philosopher: they both had chameleon-like eyes. In what his followers dubbed 'incendiary articles', the Professor of Philosophy called the chewing gum craze 'a mania for the existential gum'. In debates, leftists and rightists argued the finer points of the issue. The former were of the opinion that teeth were a metaphor for the human race while gum represented time, whereas the pessimistic rightists, or 'nihilists' as the leftists called them, upheld the view that the gum stood for human existence, while the teeth were eternity and the act of mastication a motion that would continue ad infinitum.

Our hero had nothing to do with philosophy or gum. He was an abandoned lover, standing beside a tree in a neglected park, unable to see anything but his beloved as she walked away in the rain, her black hair and red shawl fluttering gently in the wind. If it had not been for a pair of lovers from the Philosophy Department, then his presence would have remained undiscovered. They had come upon him by chance. The boy had chucked his copy of Being and Nothingness at him, causing hundreds of flies to swarm up, their buzzing increasing as the girl threw her copy of The Flies into the fray. Eventually the flies settled back onto the face of our abandoned hero. Thus, he was discovered by the brooding world of philosophy. If not for those two lovers, he would have remained a necessary philosophical ideal, for no one could grasp his existence or meaning and, naturally, his own existence couldn't grasp that of chewing gum.

At the time he wrote his articles, the Professor of Philosophy was, to our hero's good fortune, endorsing the rightist side of the debate. He rushed to the scene to examine this philosophical specimen and concluded that our hero supported his premise with regard to the tumultuousness of the human condition. The Professor of Philosophy delivered his truth as though he were a Buddha among his disciples. He circled his specimen seven times in a state of disgust and ecstasy, myopically observing the rubbish strewn all over the ground and the clear sky above. Pointing to his specimen, he exclaimed, 'Students! Write this down in your notebooks! Chewing is infinite!' The girl wept and the boy experienced an overwhelming desire to kill himself. The Professor of Philosophy left the scene with his head bowed in thought, contemplating the sky with one eye and willfully ignoring the rubbish with the other.

Not long after she disappeared into the rain, abandoning our hero beneath the tree, our heroine succumbed to the gum-chewing fad. She returned home every day with a fresh stash of gum. After locking the door, taking a bath and rubbing fragrant oils into her body, she would lie down on her bed to savour the gum. It became her most pleasurable pastime. She would slowly remove its enticing wrapper and, with a delicious shiver of anticipation, slide it through her lips as her tongue slowly licked its sweet sugary coating. She would carefully bite into it before chewing slowly and luxuriously. This private ritual allowed her to experience the mimesis of eternal repetition. She alternated libidinously between lemon, mint, apple and any of the new flavours that came onto the market. The act of mastication affirmed her femininity and offered her an intense sense of fulfillment.

Acquiring the gum was undoubtedly a challenge. She found herself in contact with people she would never otherwise have known. The scarcity of gum drove her into the arms of fixers, flight attendants, pilots, businessmen, security personnel, officers in the National Guard and numerous others. All for the sake of gum.

Another Beginning to Our Story

If my memory doesn't fail me, it started in the park. Our heroine, Fatma, stares into space. She comes from a middle class family and is studying sociology at the university. Our hero, Mukhtar, is from an established upper-class family, that enjoyed all the ease and prestige brought by power and wealth. His father is a high-ranking officer in the Royal Police Force. They sit in silence. He stretches his long legs as she hunches further into the red bench. He doesn't say a word and she doesn't leave. He can tell she belongs to a common family, an easy catch. His proximity causes her great anguish, as the attentions of affluent young men often do.

She gets up. He stands and gazes into her eyes in search of that glimmer of interest that girls often try to hide by averting their eyes. As he continues to stare into her eyes, Fatma doesn't fully turn her gaze away. Despite the absence of obvious interest, her deep black eyes and her un-coquettish behaviour captivate him. She takes a step back and he takes one forward. The dance fascinates him. She is short. In fact, everything about her is small. In some ways, she appears no older than a school girl. He longs to bury his face in her neck and hair. But her steady gaze causes him to hesitate. Unyieldingly, she continues to follow his eyes as they attempt to decipher any sign of secret longings.

He realizes that although she comes from one of those middle-class families that have, as his father would say, roamed the earth since the beginning of time, she was not an easy catch. Boys from his background assumed that sexual success was a God-given privilege. Her reticence makes her unattainable and therefore desirable. He fantasizes about her rushing towards him, her rich black hair flying around her smiling face while he, on his knees, extends his arms to hold her small body and bury his face in her neck and hair.

But, in the coming days, as they get to know one other, all these fantasies come to a stop. She keeps him at arm's length, shaking his hand as she would a stranger's. If only her small palm would indicate her formidable resilience was nearing collapse!

She stands her ground. The image of her hair billowing as she runs forever towards him, plays again and again in his mind. He waits to meet her every day under the shade of the Dakheliyyah Arches. In summer, the genius of its Italian architect shields him from the powerful desert sun, while in winter it protects him from Tripoli's erratic downpours. His fascination with her leads to an interest in the architecture around him. She would take him to the park. He would take her to the museum where they could enjoy some privacy behind its large Roman statues. He would try in vain to embrace her, but she would push him away and move nimbly amongst the figures of stone, away from his futile attempts to snatch a kiss, chattering on about social mobility and demonstrating her capacity for regurgitating university lectures.

At this point, Mukhtar found himself face to face with the statue that would mark a turning point in his life. Carved in the nineteenth century, it lay neglected against a wall in the Red Palace Museum. The statue is of a woman, her head thrown back, her eyes closed and her lips pursed as if waiting for a kiss. In our hero's eyes, this stone woman is the most lifelike sculpture in the museum, the entire city even. It was only a matter of time before his feet found their way to that statue. In its presence, he experienced an epiphany, which affected him more deeply than he could ever have imagined.

The Statue

The statue's story is one of pain and longing. It was carved by an Italian prisoner, whom the Pasha of Tripoli had kept in his dungeons for many years. The Italians ignored his work, as did the British, the Royalists and the Revolutionaries. The Italians were in search of military glory in Libya, and the British were uninterested in the historical legacy of a burdensome country they were only too happy to hand over to the Senussis, who, in turn, proclaimed all statues and statue makers as fodder for Gehenna. Had it not been for an agreement they'd reached with the Italians, they would have demolished every statue in the city immediately after Independence. Meanwhile, the Revolutionaries were torn between a hatred of imperialist Rome and its idols and an understanding of the importance of statues as representations of the glorious achievements of the Arab nation. They were both for and against statues. Roman sculptures were idolatrous, but Phoenician and modern Arab sculptures were high art.

When the prison guards discovered their Italian captive chiselling away, they immediately notified the Pasha so that he might put a stop to this most sinful of acts. If the Pasha had been in one of his more fanatical moods, he might have ordered the prisoner to be burnt alive, along with his unfinished statue. As it was, he ignored the matter and the Italian was left to carve his own road to Gehenna. Many years later, soldiers from Sicily came across the finished piece in the first days of the occupation and the sculpture was installed in a corner of the Red Palace. Convinced Libya was a nation of heathens, one Italian soldier resolved to destroy this 'idol', imagining himself a saviour. Had it not been for a second soldier, the statue would have been smashed and Mukhtar would have lost his existential compass. The Sicilian who interrupted his comrade's sudden destructive impulse requested that he be given the statue. Each and every night, he would creep up to the stone woman, kiss her lips and pleasure himself in front of her.

The soldier eventually went mad and was killed by one of his comrades after being discovered roaming around the Red Palace unabashedly naked. He couldn't have controlled his compulsive masturbation even if his military commander had barked out an order to attack the enemy. He was, nonetheless, buried with honours and the statue was shunted to a more remote corner of the Palace. However, thanks to teams of Italian archaeologists, the statue was eventually restored to the light of day. They arrived in Libya in search of Roman ruins and installed the statue in a more fitting location in the Palace. The sculpture was worthless compared to any genuine Roman military artefacts buried in the Saharan oases.

Under the British, and subsequently the Senussi monarchy, the statue remained where the Italians left it. No one noticed it except for a single Libyan guard, who also became obsessed with it. He couldn't understand why all women were not as beautiful as her. As the days went by, the guard gradually lost interest in his wife and, on Sundays, after drinking himself into a stupor, he would harass Italian women in front of the church. He ended up spending a short spell in a mental asylum, after which he began to roam the public parks, becoming a regular nuisance to Italian women and the police. Many years later, American soldiers took a picture of one of their own men kissing the statue. In his clumsy drunkenness, the soldier almost knocked it over.

After the revolution, museum officials paid scant attention to the statue, letting it stay where it was. Later, they decided to ship it off to Leptis Magna along with the statue of Septimius Severus. However, they changed their minds at the last minute and Septimius returned to his birthplace alone. As a work of art, the statue defied any recognizable aesthetic, whether Roman, Greek or Islamic. It simply had no connection to any historical era. As one sarcastic writer commented, the statue was 'like an orphan bastard!'

Nevertheless, the unknown Italian, who had been captured by Libyan sailors in the nineteenth century, was apparently quite talented and clearly knew a lot about sculpture. Perhaps he was a misguided romantic who had traveled to Libyan shores in search of adventure, hoping to lose himself there in the manner of his predecessors, who had breathlessly plowed their way towards the light, shadow and myth of the Sahara. Had he been a pirate, a trader or a spy, he would have been ransomed, as was the custom in the days of the Turkish Pashas.

The stone woman, with her closed eyes, eager lips and her face thrown back in surrender, appeared brazen; a strange and rare combination of Michelangelo's David and Da Vinci's Mona Lisa. The prisoner clearly had a lot of time on his hands in the Red Palace. Perhaps he worked as a gardener or a custodian. He must have had access to the Roman or Greek sculptures, as how else could he have obtained the necessary materials? It is possible he had managed to get hold of some Roman stone arches, which the Turks regularly used to construct their mosques and palaces. This last option seems the most plausible. It seems unlikely that the Red Palace housed any other stone artefacts during its occupation by the Turks in the nineteenth century. In a sense, the statue embarked on its own journey through time. Unknown and almost forgotten, it destroyed whomever knew of its existence. But otherwise it remained in the dark, metaphorically and literally, even for the custodians of the Red Palace who encountered it on a daily basis.

Mukhtar was one of the many destined to see his life entangled with it. The day he found himself face to face with the stone woman while pursuing Fatma amongst the giant Roman statues, he was left spellbound by the brazen readiness of this female form and the eagerness of its lips. Nevertheless, Fatma remained the focus of his desire. Her energy, her rich dark hair, flying in the wind, her body, flowing with life as she moved towards him, made her the living embodiment of desire. Otherwise, he would have surrendered to the stone woman, he would have remained spellbound, hugging and kissing the statue until, like many before him, they dragged him away to the asylum. But Fatma's approaching form distracted him, most likely saving him from such a fate.

He would spread his arms as if to hug the stone woman. It was as though she were running towards him without ever reaching him, while he could never bring himself to embrace her. From that fateful moment, long before the Professor of Philosophy returned from France, his existence could be summed up as a slow succumbing to the fate of the 'existential gum.'

The Park

Mukhtar would take her to the museum and Fatma would take him to the park. These were the places where they could talk and get to know one another in the intimacy of the silence. The park was in a state of neglect: empty cartons and cigarette stubs, the idle men, the drug addicts, the drunks, the dealers and the police raids. Yet it was a welcoming hide-out for our museum lovers. She would drag him to the park, wipe the red bench with her handkerchief and ask him to sit down. She felt the warmth of his soul as his eyes continued to desire her body. She tidied their private space amidst the general neglect, collecting and discarding the cigarette stubs from around and beneath their chairs, planting flowers and bringing water to nurse the new shoots. She never despaired, no matter how many times she had to replant the flowers, which were flattened and trampled by the drunks and deadbeats who slept in the park at night. She would rest against the red bench with her eyes closed, breathing in the smell of the grass and the trees, longing for a kiss that never arrived.

Unlike the statue, the park was representative of the many historical eras that Tripoli had witnessed. It was farmland originally, sustaining countless generations of impoverished peasants who were eventually forced to sell it to a governor during the Turkish rule. He turned the land into a pleasure park for summer parties, filling it with drummers, musicians, dancers and jugglers. The Pashas engaged in all manner of pleasures over the years and the park's grass soaked up the lascivious sweat of Europeans, Africans and Turks, mixed with the heady vapours of rich wines. The loud neighing of horses and the relentless moaning of slave girls drove the birds away. The bodies of women were seen dangling from the trees where they had ended their lives after being violated by Turkish soldiers. Many a cajoling poet, hailing from some far flung corner of the world, would walk into these gatherings and sell his flattery and praise. The park was a familiar scene for wild zar gatherings, playing host to the dancing and skullduggery of charlatans in Sufi garb and often ambushed by desperate women, betrayed by their philandering Pasha husbands.

The park was overhauled many times, destroyed by revolutions, Bedouin raids and European naval assaults on Tripoli. The sea submerged it five times, as did countless rainstorms. These calamities claimed their share of victims: drummers, musicians, charlatans, dancers, whores, soldiers, government workers, tribal sheikhs and even Pashas. According to popular lore, at night the park becomes crowded with the souls of the dead: the suicides and the murdered wives of vengeful husbands. The ghost of one Turkish officer is often seen chasing a Pasha, who is naked except for his tarboosh. The Pasha is said to have seduced the officer's wife when he was away collecting taxes. The Pasha was eventually caught making love on the grass with the officer's wife, who escaped across the fields without a stitch on her. The officer was shot by his own men before he could pursue her.

It is said the Italian gunships put an end to the Pasha's pleasure park when they bombarded the city. It became the scene of fierce combat between the Libyans and

Italians. The earth soaked up their blood and, despite so many deaths, wild red poppies and white daisies bloomed. Their heady odour filled the air, mingling with the smell of blood gushing from fresh wounds. The beauty of the flowers couldn't, however, tempt any Libyan to approach the park. A naked Turkish woman was often seen roaming there at night, but she was found dead during the fourth year of the occupation. After quelling the resistance, the Italians, as the latest wave of occupiers, began dividing Tripoli into zones as though it were an Italian city. Police stations, government buildings, bars, casinos, theatres, museums and factories appeared, until it bore all the features of an Italian city. The remains of the Pasha's nocturnal pleasure park were landscaped according to Italian tastes and redesigned to fit their urban sensibilities. Hundreds of Libyans, with their camels and donkeys, were conscripted to level the land and plow the surface. The park became worthy of any Italian city. Tripoli, after all, was the capital of their vaunted Quarta Sponda, or Fourth Shore, facing the toe of the Italian shoe that remained suspended over history, afraid to get wet in the waters of the Mediterranean basin.

Very few Libyans ventured into the park. The Italian police forbade vagabonds and beggars from loitering there, but certain young men chose to mingle with the Italian settlers, mimicking their style and ways of life. They were known as New Libyans. Had it not been for the dark colour of their skin and their tarbooshes, one would have thought they were genuine Italians. The New Libyans were poets, sons of traders and employees of the occupying government, both those with political aspirations and informants working for the secret service. The park became a genuinely Italian space except for a few palm trees, a scattering of Libyan workers and the New Libyans. Otherwise, a visitor would have thought he was standing in a park in Italy.

Amazingly, the park was spared the devastation of World War II and it remained a secluded corner during the first years of the British occupation. The only people who frequented it were Libyan prostitutes in native dress. Each lady signaled her availability by chewing gum loudly and rapidly until she caught the attention of a potential client, at which point she would slow the pace of mastication. Most of them preferred British soldiers, although some remained partial to the local clientele. The park remained quiet during the British administration except for the murder of a prostitute at the hands of her male cousin. He came from the village looking for her and found her in the park. Having carefully tracked her movements, he stabbed her to death before pulling a gun on nearby demonstrators calling for Libyan independence. The British, in turn, began firing on the crowds, killing yet more people. These incidents aside, the park adhered to the so-called 'British peace', becoming a place for derelicts, political activists, and, of course, prostitutes, tirelessly chewing their gum.

The plot against Libyan Independence was somewhat derailed when the Haitian representative to the United Nations made a drunken mistake. According to a tacit, prearranged agreement, he was not supposed to lift his hand for or against Libya's national independence, but unwittingly did so. His vote acted as the tie-breaker in favour of Libyan Independence. In an instant, this drunken act accomplished more than could ever have been plotted and hatched behind closed doors. One of the streets behind the park was eventually named Adrian Pelt Street, after the UN High Commissioner who had recommended independence for Libya. The name of the Haitian representative was, however, sadly omitted from the list of names put forward for honorific 'independence streets'. The Senussi government eventually made their peace with the alcohol merchants, even after seeing firsthand the consequence of their trade when it came to Libya's national fate. Situated next to Adrian Pelt Street, the park remained relatively peaceful during the early years of Independence, despite the regular police raids on prostitutes. These operations didn't seek to abolish prostitution, but merely establish order in the country. Prostitution was consigned to special areas, such as the street named after the famous Arab philosopher al-Kindi that, prior to Independence, was known as Via Galduni. During the war, however, prostitutes abandoned al-Kindi Street for the park. After Independence, such a line of work no longer seemed appropriate as the new government strove to establish a modern nation.

The park was the main arena for the decade-long raids on prostitutes. Mukhtar had been told about one incident in particular: the bloody confrontation that took place between the Royal Police and the students who were massacred after daring to pelt stones at law enforcement officers. At the time, Mukhtar's father was an enthusiastic police officer, loyal to the King and invested in protecting the stability of his rule. In a moment of intense indignation, he took the decision to shoot at the students. In return, he suffered severe head injuries and his hat, with its royal yellow insignia fell to the ground, where he lay bleeding. Mukhtar's father still managed to enjoy unusual vigour despite being imprisoned by the Revolutionaries as they conducted an inquiry into all the police files of the Royal period. Although it had been many years since the park shootings, he still hated the place, which brought back memories of young bodies bleeding and falling. As he tended his farm, the scene would play repeatedly in his mind, saddening him and filling him with dread, even though he was remorseless.

Neglect turned the park into a rubbish dump after the nationalization of the Sanitation Company. The bankrupt public sector lacked the manpower to undertake a project of such complexity. In their excessive romanticism, the Revolutionaries thought it beneath the dignity of any decent Libyan to collect rubbish. How could a newly liberated citizen be a rubbish collector? At the same time, wasting financial resources on importing foreign labour went against the revolutionary principle of self-sufficiency. The park found itself at a crossroads between reality and utopia. Despite this neglect, the park became a refuge for all types of visitors. Intellectuals went there to read, poets to recite, lovers to whisper and hashish dealers to trade their wares. Surprisingly, the alcohol merchants didn't do much business. Very few arrests took place and, against all odds, the park remained a municipal garden.

——— ✿✿✿✿✿ ———

The Father

Omar Effendi, as Tripoli had come to know Mukhtar's father in the 1960s, was not a native of the city. He arrived as a policeman and the British employed him throughout the fifties, as did the Royalists after that. He loved the King and considered him a holy man, a marabout, as the Libyans say. Omar Effendi was not particularly religious; he drank alcohol and was one of the more frequent customers of al-Kindi Street at the beginning of his professional life. Nonetheless, he had deep faith in the baraka, or divine blessing, of the King, and continued to fast during Ramadan and to attend the Friday prayers. He was a man of contradictions, consuming so much alcohol on a Thursday night that he would pass out and yet still rise the following day to perform his ablutions and attend the prayers with genuine piety. This paradox became a pattern. He could brutally shoot down students and still sob bitterly at the sight of dead bodies in a traffic accident.

Omar Effendi was not a broad-shouldered man, nor did he have a strong constitution as one would imagine a police officer should. He was tall, dark and slender, with an unwavering loyalty to the soul of the King and his 'blessed reign', which endured even after the monarchy was abolished. Despite the decent treatment he received from the Revolutionaries, who could easily have killed him with the full support of the masses, he didn't warm to them, regarding them as commoners unfit for government. They allowed him to keep his farm, his mansion and his rank, and even provided him with financial assistance. His intense dislike and disdain of the Revolution and its perpetrators didn't prevent him from enjoying these privileges that, for some strange reason, seemed to exceed those enjoyed by certain Revolutionaries.

At seventy, Omar Effendi's inconsistencies continued. He kept up his Thursday night drinking parties only to wake up the following morning and attend the prayers. This routine started at the time of the Revolution, when he left the city and relocated to his farm, leaving behind his wife and only son, Mukhtar. While at his farm, he began to nurse a new infatuation for the young generation of easy girls, inviting them to his soirées of music and Eastern dance. Omar Effendi's taste in women underwent a dramatic change in his later years. Large women ceased to appeal to him, with their sagging arms and enormous breasts where he had once loved to bury his face. He began to spend his evenings with slim attractive girls, skilled at belly dancing, an arrangement managed by a prostitute named Ghouiliya.

Omar Effendi first met Ghouiliya in the late sixties when she was just a regular street girl. She was slim and dark in those days. As she didn't have many customers, she ran errands for other prostitutes and their pimps. Omar Effendi thus sought her help to provide him with girls and liquor, which became his most important considerations in retirement. The girls would arrive every Thursday after sundown at Omar Effendi's farm. He would emerge much later, spending the first hour of the evening in the private company of Ghouiliya. No one knew what took place between them. Some girls said that she plied him with stimulants concocted from almonds and honey, or that she massaged certain parts of his body to stimulate blood flow and desire. Others said that this was when she settled her accounts for the evening. Ghouiliya's closest friend said that she accomplished all three tasks in that one hour. As the soirée progressed, Omar Effendi would be seen dancing and balancing his wine glass on his head. The evening would end when he dragged one of the girls off to his bedroom, where he would strip her clothes off and fall asleep with his head nestled between her hot thighs while she exhaled her alcoholic breath between his cold legs. He would often dream of regressing, returning to a sperm-like form, floating through a warm, safe darkness. The following day, he would get up by mid-morning, wash his body, perfume it with musk and amber, and dress completely in white. In his prayers, he would ask for mercy and forgiveness for all that had taken place the night before.

Ten years went by in this manner until our heroine arrived at the farm for the first time, having abandoned both our hero's love and her education. She was still shrouded in her black coat and red shawl and chewing lemon-flavoured gum. And she, in turn, was being chewed up by a great emptiness. When she had left the park, she had abandoned her own soul with our hero. Her body had felt like a small hollow barrel, bumping noisily down the street. Without having to call for it, a taxi pulled up beside her and she told him to go 'where the money was.' In silence, he drove her to Ghouiliya. After an inspection in which her breasts were thoroughly prodded and squeezed, Ghouiliya gave Fatma and the taxi driver fifty dinars each and dragged her into the mansion by yanking on her shawl.

She didn't feel uncomfortable entering an unknown place. The advance had put her mind at ease and she realized how relatively simple the game was. She was in a hurry and wanted matters to end quickly. She asked where the bedroom was. Without a word, Ghouiliya led her to a spacious room decorated in pink. She sat on the edge of the bed in order to avoid catching sight of herself in the mirror and then lay back with her eyes closed, waiting for a customer whom she knew would most likely be her father's age. The 'punter' – according to the taxi driver – was an elderly man who would not physically hurt her or harm her reputation. It would not go further than light petting. She waited a long time. She considered getting up and heading back to the park where our hero was waiting in the rain. She thought of retracing her steps to that moment when her soul had felt like it was seeping away. But she changed her mind, trying to keep focused on her present adventure.

Her new plan was to save at least one thousand dollars and travel to Turkey to stock up on gum, which she would then re-sell for three times the price. Such trips would rake in a quarter of a million dinars, which she could put towards a house, a car, and eventually an independent lifestyle with no family constraints, where she would be free to marry whomever she wished. These thoughts flashed through her mind and began to sound like a viable plan. Mukhtar was strange and unpredictable, and their relationship had begun to frighten her. Chasing him every single day among the statues of the museum was crazy. She knew she had to leave and relinquish the repetitive cycle of visiting museum and park. She must completely disappear from his life. She had to quit university and take a quick, decisive step up the social ladder. She knew it was a dangerous move, a gamble that could jeopardize all her dreams. Nevertheless, she took the plunge and was encouraged by the taxi that stopped without her signaling. It was as if the car were a sign, an angelic being that would instantaneously transport her from one life to another. Contrary to all the sociological theories she had laboriously memorized, her drive towards mobility was sudden, unplanned and unexpected. She quit university, her lover and her family in one fell swoop.

Fatma didn't arrive at the farm on a Thursday and she found Omar Effendi unprepared to entertain a woman. He had just completed his sunset prayers and was wearing his long white jilbab, resembling a religious ascetic who had rejected the pleasures of the body. He walked into the bedroom, unaware of her presence. Seeing her there, he managed to greet her as though he knew her and found her presence there perfectly natural. She waited for him to draw near and touch her hand, to greet her the way a man must greet a woman he finds in his bedroom. It surprised her that he treated her as though she were his little daughter, asking her what was the matter and placing his hand on her shoulder to ease her fear. But she wasn't afraid at all. After all, she was in a rush and had removed her black coat without taking off her red shawl. She turned her face towards him with her eyes closed. Startled by this gesture, he flinched unwittingly and calmly asked her what she wanted. Without waiting for an answer, he pulled a hundred dinar note from the pocket of his jilbab and tucked it into her cleavage, whispering that she should come back on Thursday night. She picked up her black coat and left the room and the farm. No one spoke to her on the way out. She found the taxi waiting for her. Silently and without asking for directions, the taxi driver took her back to the park. As she stepped out of the car he said, 'Thursday then,' and drove off.

After our heroine left, Omar Effendi wished he could have made an exception and that she had stayed. She was probably a virgin. Everything about her was small. He looked around. It was as if the glow of youth filled the room. The smell of her young warm body lingered on the bed. He lay back, feeling its imprint as the details of that mesmerizing first encounter pulsed through his mind. He was obsessed with young girls. Their short stature and small breasts stirred his lustful, seventy-year old soul. Fatma fulfilled his every desire. It even crossed his mind to find her and ask her to marry him, which is what usually happens when a rich man meets a poor young girl in melodramatic Arabic films. He would have granted her every wish had she stayed and allowed him to inhale the scent of life pulsing from her small body. But she had left because he didn't ask her to stay. Like in Arabic films, the father doesn't know the girl he desires is the one for whom his only son is waiting in the rain. The heroine, in turn, doesn't know that the man she went to meet and to whom she offered her small body, is also the father of her deserted lover. In this way, our story follows a roughly Arabic template, diverging, on one hand, from the late Egyptian writer Ihsan Abd al-Qaddus's The Vacant Pillow but closely resembling another of his novels, The Well of Deprivation, where the heroine prostitutes herself as ours does, but unconsciously, as if in a trance. Fatma, on the other hand, is conscious of her actions and doesn't conduct her affairs at night. Our heroine forges ahead in broad daylight.

The Story of Our Heroine

Fatma came from a conservative family. Her father was an employee in the Ministry of Religious Affairs. Hers was one of those humble families who had benefited greatly from the socialist revolution. They were able to move into flats built by Poles, Bulgarians and Egyptians and become familiar with modern luxuries like fridges, telephones and gramophones. The families were given opportunities in terms of education, employment and loans. Such benefits allowed them, like the old-moneyed class, to own and appreciate such pleasures as bananas, honey, cassette tapes and other fashionable items. They travelled to Europe and America for tourism and education. They experienced this new good life in the seventies and came to believe in the Revolution, in Nasserism and in Arab Nationalism. Our heroine's generation was infatuated with Farid al-Atrash and, of course, Abd al-Halim Hafez. They lived like the Nasserite bourgeoisie and, like its poor, they chanted its slogans. In short – and avoiding any novelistic pretention – one could say that our heroine's upbringing provided the perfect conditions for The Well of Deprivation. The Well of Deprivation is an Egyptian novel our heroine didn't read, nor did she see the Egyptian actress, Soad Hosny, play the leading role in the film version. Despite all her progress, our heroine had never been to the cinema. She had only watched a few conservative Egyptian films on television, which had been produced long before The Well of Deprivation. Nevertheless, our heroine played the same role as Soad Hosny. Her thirst caused her to travel off into the night, in search of values, ethics and social status.

At the beginning of our narrative, when our hero brought his mouth close to Fatma's ear, she was by all accounts an innocent girl. She would, undoubtedly, have come to experience at least one of those nights Ihsan Abd al-Qaddus describes in The Well of Deprivation. Instead, those ten long years were spent chewing gum and moving from one farm to another and one rest-stop to the next. During those years, her father committed suicide on learning of his daughter's scandalous lifestyle, followed a month later by her mother. Our heroine's brother isolated himself in their flat and abandoned his revolutionary work against bourgeois exploitation. In the process, he relinquished all his beliefs in an egalitarian society, socialism, justice and moral rectitude, opting for a life as a simple employee, becoming a social misfit in the fast-paced world of networking.

In The Well of Deprivation, the heroine leads two contradictory lifestyles. By day she is the daughter of a conservative bourgeois family and by night, she escapes from the window, wearing the revealing outfits of prostitutes, to engage in libidinous sexual adventures. All these nocturnal events happen unconsciously. It is only the following morning that she discovers the tell-tale signs of the previous night on her body. The story concerns a sexual awakening that takes place when the soul is asleep, relieving its owner of all feelings of guilt and vulgarity.

Our heroine experiences a similar well of deprivation in another country and another time. Unlike Abd al-Qaddus's heroine, Fatma is well aware of her actions.

She knowingly sells her body, and she is not surprised by the markings of her red nights the following morning. But, like the heroine in Abd al-Qaddus's novel, she walks down the street in modest clothes, with eyes downcast, ignoring the catcalls. Until she encounters a customer, she comes across as serious and conservative. She develops the ability to spot and size up her clients amidst large crowds. Then she begins to chew her gum more nervously and vigorously to attract his attention, and slows her chewing down after that. She would continue chewing expansively until an agreement was reached, after which she would continue on her way with downcast eyes.

What was interesting about these transactions was that our heroine didn't enjoy being with men. What she really loved were those moments of highly charged, expansive chewing. The outward signs of her arousal during intercourse were all simulated. It was as though sex were an act committed by an angry soul, not unlike murder or bodily mutilation. The coital act would end with her violently hugging the client and drowning him in hot tears. One could conclude that her relationship to gum was the only thing that allowed her to feel her femininity after she left our hero in the rain ten years ago. But chewing gum was not a novel experience for her, and had not always been charged with such significance. At first, it was simply a way of passing time before she enrolled in the Sociology department and grew obsessed with social mobility, long before meeting Mukhtar and sitting beside him on the red park bench.

When he took her to the museum and saw the statue, she was struck by its aura of femininity, hedonism and surrender. Every time she attempted to kiss him amongst the large Roman sculptures, or embrace him beneath the Dakheliyyah Arches, the image of that statue would come between them. The sculpture was the curse that drove her away. She was intelligent enough to know that Mukhtar was lost, that he was looking for the image of the sculpture in her and that he needed an idol, whilst she needed movement. So she left him, motionless, in the rain.

The gum began to embody the truest experience of love and sex for her, the sense of being and renewal she had desired from the moment she left the park. The gum became the only companion with whom she could truly engage. All of this was beyond the consciousness of anyone influenced by the ideas of the Professor of Philosophy. Although it was a subject related to her university studies, she had never given philosophy or Sartre much thought. Gum was simply a pleasure and nothing else. Unwrapping the gum, feeling it against her lips, becoming conscious of her own soft, sticky saliva as her tongue touched its smooth surface before drawing it inward as its sweetness filled her mouth, all of this made her experience a plenitude that one can equate with pleasure, a twitching that she knew well, but that had no associations with any man in particular. Far from the theories of the Professor of Philosophy, Fatma, a girl of twenty-two summers, as she liked to describe herself, truly embodied the 'era of gum'. It was a time of endless chewing, which re-enacted the Well of Deprivation in a different mode.

———— ✿✿✿✿✿ ————

Our Hero

Mukhtar, motionless in the rain for ten years, still expected Fatma to turn around and run back to him. In a way, his life thus far had already been one long state of expectation, a constant oscillation between nervous and expansive chewing. At one moment he was a child, wearing his father's big, heavy hat with its gold insignia, being chauffeured around and observing the flustered driver open the door and, with great flourish, exclaim 'Good morning Sir!' At another, he was at the mercy of his father's Sudanese whip that hung alongside his big heavy hat. Long after he had outgrown childhood and his father had retired from the police, the older man was still liable to lash it across his son's face. His mind oscillated between those moments. Motionless under the tree, his eyes followed her as she moved further away in her black coat and red scarf, the crowning glory in his long journey of constant chewing. In other words, the decade he spent under the rain was like the wait he'd endured for the whip to come violently down on his sweaty neck, or for the hat to grace his head with all its glory. It was as if his eyes were chewing the image of Fatma's walking away, hoping she would stop, turn round and run back to him.

There he stood, as we have said, with his hair and beard growing longer, in his tattered clothes, surrounded by the kaleidoscopic litter of discarded wrappers. The discarded wrappers soon became the subject of investigative journalism, receiving their academic due from the Professor of Economics, who had recently returned from the United States, having studied Keynes and taken a disliking to him. He had, meanwhile, become completely infatuated with

Mao Zedong, but took care to conceal this predilection for fear of the CIA and the Libyan security services. In their repeated efforts to combat consumerism and capitalist values, the newspapers published several pictures of our hero surrounded by the empty wrappers. The Professor of Economics, though aware of his students' ignorance of English, made excessive use of the language. Gleaning the subject from the press, he gave it an academic patina, as he always liked to say, with a detailed graph, mapping the evolution of consumerism in Libya according to the type and country of origin of the wrappers. Used as a dating technique, the wrappers traced consumerist trends in Libya. There were Italian, French, German, American, Swiss and Danish wrappers, as well as Tunisian, Egyptian, Turkish and, of course, Chinese, Taiwanese, Bulgarian and Yugoslavian ones. The Taiwanese wrappers, with their faded nationalist colours, were somewhere in the middle of his scale. The Professor of Economics concluded that Libyan consumerism was essentially directed by political exigencies, although he didn't disclose this in his pioneering survey.

After having been the Professor of Philosophy's prized specimen, our hero became the subject of interest to yet another vaunted thinker of the realm, a Theatre Director recently returned from Hungary. The image of our hero bending to pick up one of the wrappers resembled, in the eyes of the Theatre Director, a Greek god plucking Ulysses's ship from a raging storm. Our hero thus mesmerized the Theatre Director, who continued to chew on the scene for ten whole years. His project stalled due to lack of funds and the Theatre Director eventually became part of the park himself. He would come every day and sit opposite our hero, pondering the finer existential details of the gum. The Theatre Director was oblivious to the visits of the Professor of Economics and his students as they closely examined the litter. The two men were, in turn, unaware of the visits of the Professor of Philosophy. Naturally, our hero saw nothing except our heroine as she moved away in her black coat and red shawl. He stood under the tree in the middle of the park for a whole decade, conscious only of the growing distance between them.

Life in the park continued as it always had, lovers came and went, as did poets: some would write and others would talk to the wind and leave. The police monitored that too. Thus the park continued to be home to prostitutes, pimps, drug dealers, politicians, johns, pickpockets and insomniacs vainly trying to sleep in the open air – all of whom were kept under constant surveillance by the police, who continued to chew over their own activities. All these strangers came and went while our hero stood motionless under the tree, waiting for her to turn around and come back to him, for ten long years. It had only taken twenty-four hours, which barely amounted to a single moment in our hero's conception of time, before High Command was flooded by over a hundred security reports detailing our hero's motionless presence and presenting photographs as supporting evidence.

By the time thirty-six hours had elapsed, a special Security Squad, composed of members of different departments and headed by one of our hero's university colleagues, was dispatched to the scene. For an entire year, the squad monitored his coordinates, occupying the premises of a security company that displayed, as a front, the banner of a boutique, and looked onto the park. Should our hero have taken a step in any direction, he would have set off a security alert, forcing the squad to relocate to another monitoring base.

Unlike the Security Squad, the Revolutionaries analyzed our hero's situation as a discourse on class. The wealthy son of a prominent Royal Police Officer was a potent symbol. They saw him as a genuine example of a reactionary trend. He displayed the rigidity of the deteriorating Royal era and, unlike all the other statues constructed at the time, he didn't cost a penny! Precise and original, here stood a form that the most accomplished of sculptors could never have achieved, and that symbolized an important and dangerous transitional period of Libyan history. To the Revolutionaries, our hero was irrefutable evidence of the filth of consumerism. He was a living symbol, much debated in newspapers, academic studies and television programmes. In the eyes of our Revolutionaries, he was a museum piece, a relic of capitalist values. Closer to the truth would be that our hero was chasing the mirage of a blue beam of light across a long dark night. He was attracted by its gleam as our heroine moved further away in the rain, shrouded in her black coat and red shawl. He was trying to hold fast to the last glimpses of light, to the edge of the sunset as she moved away. He was trying to stay the course before the start of that blackest of nights.

——— ✧✧✧✧✧ ———

The Night Mirage

The night mirage our hero chased for ten years beneath a tree in the park was a numinous blue hue that overshadowed the blinding noon of Tripoli. The mirage spread its light in the darkness, giving the city a soft wet ambiance. As Fatma walked away in her black coat and red shawl, it was as if her coat covered the noon sun and her shawl dispersed the heat across the darkest part of the sky. The slow motion of her departing steps imbued Tripoli with diaphanous textures.

While I was writing the above scene, our heroine was posing naked on an old couch in the house of a painter attempting to draw her in the European style. She was the first naked woman he had laid eyes on, which perhaps explained his flustered movements. She wanted to end the session, so she rose, moved towards him, clasped her arms around his neck and kissed him on the mouth. She slowly started to undo his shirt, one button at a time, and finally left him on the floor amidst his tussled trousers, after pocketing the one hundred dinars they had agreed upon. During ten long years, he had painted more than one hundred pictures, all of which tried to capture the same image. The curtains of his studio were drawn and the light seemed to stand still as she moved towards him. He, too, chased the mirage of that image for ten long years.

She walked out on the painter as he lay on the floor, a victim whose mouth had come so close to pleasure without ever having tasted it. She went to the café to look for her next customer before it got dark and the deals of the night were concluded. At the café, there were as many customers as there were girls, all chewing their gum slowly and nervously, conducting their negotiations with studied calm and determination. Fatma was just thinking of turning back as she entered the door, when she caught sight of a potential customer, looking anxious in his seat. He stood up the moment he saw her and smiled as she headed towards his table. He called her Reem, or sometimes Maryam or Zaynab. He never asked her what her real name was, nor did he reveal his own. The other couple of times he went out with her, he had directly asked how much she wanted, to which she had replied 'One hundred dinars.' He would laugh and say 'Two hundred then!' and recite bawdy poems until they arrived at his farmstead in Wadi al-Rabi.

It was there that she carried out her exhausting work, forcing her tiny body to absorb the shock of her explosive customer. At the start of his assault, he would call her Reem then, as he crushed her small breasts with his large head, he would call her Maryam and, as he collapsed on top of her, shaking and moaning, he would call her Zaynab. She would scream until she passed out. On regaining consciousness, she would find him crying on her chest, begging for forgiveness. Thanks to the other girls, Fatma found out that he was an important building contractor for schools, hospitals, army barracks and prisons. He owned many farms and villas, rarely spending two consecutive nights in any one place. He moved between places and women, and our heroine became his latest fancy. He was infatuated with her short height and small breasts, a preference not unusual amongst her rich older clients. Inflicting pain on a small frame, the screaming, the shaking of small breasts and the sight of bite marks on short necks apparently satisfied their aggressive sexuality. As she walked away from the customer, the mirage would spread out and descend, like night, on everything around him.

This night mirage, with its soft blue hue, imparted a poetic atmosphere to an age of coarseness and superficiality. The Theatre Director referred to it as visual poetics, as he called all the blue lit night scenes that dominated his one and only work, which took a full year to produce, and was performed for one night only to a small number of friends. Despite his failures, he described this work as a redemptive act, a salvation from superficiality and blandness. He also saw the Professor of Economics, recently returned from America, who was studying the wrappers and recording observations. The Theatre Director was not interested either in our hero, the Professor of Economics or the Professor of Philosophy. He was interested only in his colleague, the Director recently returned from Hungary. He chewed him over and over again in blue lit scenes that communicated nothing but an impression of blueness and a vacant staring into the void. The Theatre Director was oblivious to the security patrol, which spotted him and took multiple photographs. The most important of these managed to capture the image of all the Professors and all the Directors, returned from all of their different destinations. It somewhat resembled a Salvador Dalí painting. The first Director appears, observing the Director recently returned from Hungary, who in turn is observing our hero, followed by the Professor of Economics recently returned from America and the

Professor of Philosophy recently returned from France. A journalist is also present, and a security agent. The security patrol considered this photograph to be the best, not knowing that they, too, were part of a larger canvas.

The night mirage chased our heroine as our hero stood beneath the tree in the park, waiting for her to stop and return to him as she always had when they met at the Dakheliyyah Arches. For ten long years, the mirage hounded the darkness as it moved closer. He yearned for her to stop, when all she wanted was to escape from the statue and the restrictions of the nineteenth century. And no one really saw him or noticed his exhaustion.

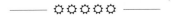

The Gum

Chewing gum can be considered a girlish act: the lifting of the tongue, the sucking, the nervous tension, the slowness. It is a subject of interest for those in media, politics and even academia. Libya is probably the first country in the world to have become so preoccupied with gum for the length of time it did, when larger international problems loomed in the background. Issues abounded – modernity, the arms race, Palestine, Arab unity, social justice, UN amendments, OPEC and the price of oil, and American and British conspiracies against Libya. Despite this, the country succeeded in taking the first leap into the postmodern world, long before any of its 'sister' Arab states, which seemed to be ostentatiously focused on headier topics. This Libyan post-modernity didn't originate from the top, but can be termed a grass roots movement. Shampoo, bananas, cassette tapes of Western music, jeans, alcohol and the rest of the postmodern inventory were 'chewed' daily on Libyan streets, in its media outlets, revolutionary councils and other state organizations. The gum forced its philosophy onto every aspect of life.

Gum was a priority for Fatma, if not her most important priority. She discovered many different flavours and got to know many people. She offered her small body to men, and found herself in unfamiliar places. She followed the debates on the radio and television and even went so far as to read the articles the Professor of Philosophy had published in an anthology that was cheaply distributed. For years to come, radio and television programmes were to chew the book's content. Our heroine would not even have read it had it not been for its title, Existence: Gum. The gum was to become her new life project as she moved away in the rain, shrouded in her black coat and red shawl, away from our hero, the statue, the park, the Red Palace, the family and the tribe. It was the gum and the chewing that allowed our heroine to regain some rhythm, some part of the feminine identity she thought she had lost.

The pure joy of chewing helped her through that decade. Her body would relax, tremble and open up, so that her soul could fly out across a transparent blue in the dark of night. The gum was her night mirage, allowing her to experience pleasure despite the pain of selling her body to gum peddlers and smugglers. Fatma abandoned her import scheme and chewed on the idea instead. She became well acquainted with middlemen, and she kept asking them questions about the ins and outs of their business, even during intercourse. For her, sex in itself was not enjoyable. Only chewing occupied that place. Chewing, of course, became trendy and it was not limited merely to women and the young. The sight of an old man enjoying his gum in front of his house was not unusual, nor even the telltale popping coming from the mouth of an old lady! The trend caught on, despite the concerted efforts of the media, the ministry of religious affairs, women's groups and youth organizations to stamp it out. These ceaseless campaigns became a form of constant churning, without the apparently virtuous warriors ever getting to enjoy the actual act of chewing!

Gum destroyed houses famous for their generosity and pride, just as it built up others on illusory foundations. Many of our heroine's newly found friends were once indigent, and yet the gum transformed them into forthright capitalists. Fatma also knew people who had lost everything as a result of gum. Throughout that decade, gum became a mirage, a translucent, blue mirage that everyone chased. It became a philosophical project, embodying aesthetic values that were translated into theatre, music, art, pop culture, doctoral dissertations in economics and political science and a classified top-secret dossier that caused much trouble to the security forces. It was debated by rightists, leftists, centre leftists, centre rightists, and so on, to no end. In brief, gum became everyone's obsession. But the actual enjoyable act of mastication remained a privilege of the few. One of whom was our heroine.

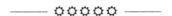

'I Chew Her and She Chews Me'

The name Rahma, which means mercy, is a name loved by Libyans. It is often given to girls whose mothers have had many sons, so that when a girl is finally born, she is seen as a merciful angel who will one day assist with the caring of her father and brothers. Rahma, whom we cannot ignore in this story, is the mother of our hero, who is still standing beneath the tree in the middle of the park. She hailed from a Turco-Libyan family and it is thought her grandfather was an Ottoman officer, as Libyans called the Turks before the Italians invaded. He was killed, leaving behind a small girl who was abandoned by her mother after she went mad following her husband's death. We have already met this mother in our story, she is the nocturnal park wanderer who disappears during the day and is found dead in the fourth year of the Italian occupation. The orphaned daughter was raised by a Libyan, who eventually married her to his son. Thus, Rahma was conceived. Rahma's blonde hair and white skin, both Turkish features, attracted Omar Effendi when he was in the Royal Police Force. She married him because of his uniform and height. His slim figure and the darkness of his skin disgusted her, however, which is probably why she only conceived one son, our hero Mukhtar.

Rahma lived alone in her husband's house on Ben Ashur Street after he sequestered himself in his farm, while her son – as we know – remained in the park, beneath the rain. She is now fifty, more or less, and has maintained her Turkish beauty as well as her feelings of disgust towards her husband. She enjoyed smoking her

hookah, a habit she picked up after the Revolution when
her husband was dismissed from the Force, imprisoned
and interrogated. She tried it for the first time in the
house of one of her Turkish friends and it soon became
her closest companion. In fact, Rahma spent ten years
enjoying her hookah in her garden without noticing her
only son's absence. Nor did she give much thought to her
husband, who had left both her and their house a long
time ago. At the beginning of every month, he would send
his wife an allowance via one of his workers, providing
her with a certain level of comfort. She maintains a
youthful appearance, highlighting her hair with blonde
streaks, and making sure that the pink of her lipstick
matches the colour of her nipples.

Smoking her hookah, Rahma waits for her friend
Uthman to return from Turkey. He contacts her upon
his arrival at Tripoli's airport. She loves how he calls
her his honeypot as he hugs her. She laughs and kisses
him coquettishly, calling him her cream pie. They spend
long hours together, mixing honey and cream, after
which they inhale their hookah until they cough long and
luxuriously. All this happened ten years ago. She was fifty
then, as she is now. Uthman had met her at the house
of a Turkish friend. At first he thought that she, too,
was Turkish, leading him to kiss her on both cheeks as
Europeans do, and awakening fifty years of thirst and
desire in her. They laughed at the mannerism, and later
exchanged bawdy jokes and promised to meet in her
house. They made love, as Europeans say, for the only
time and coughed together for long hours after. He was
one of the most important gum traders travelling back

and forth to Turkey. Somewhere along the way, however, he got lost and never came back, a circumstance that made Rahma chew on their fleeting relationship for ten long years.

Rahma was not conscious of the transformations of our other characters. The stages in her life, until she met Uthman, had been empty and fragmented. Childhood, youth, loss of virginity, unfulfilled desire and then motherhood. She harboured an ambivalent longing for the past and found the smell and touch of wet grass exhilarating, especially against her naked body. Her life felt like a long dark tunnel that threatened to blind her. She spent ten years chewing over the moments she had spent with Uthman. She sat in her garden, awaiting his arrival from the airport. The night he left, he had assured her, 'I will call you the moment I arrive in Tripoli.' She waited ten long years for a call that never came. Days, months and years went by. She was fixated on that one moment as she inhaled the smoke of her hookah.

The hookah around which Rahma's life revolved was not regarded by Libyans as originally Turkish, as the Turks claimed, but as something which they shared with their Arab brothers. It was seen as an achievement of Nasser, an emblem of Freedom, Socialism and Unity, the holy trinity that sparked the fires of Revolution in Libyans and their oil, but which ultimately and unfortunately resulted in rubbish piling up, along with inadequate housing, incompetent health services, poor education, bribery and corruption. The Egyptians, who arrived in Libya as experts in everything, introduced the hookah alongside the Revolution and it soon became a common sight in parks, streets and deserts. Urban parks began to resemble giant coffee houses packed with Egyptians and new Libyans who eagerly imitated their exotic way of life. The Libyans most attracted to the hookah were those who had visited Egypt as tourists or students, intellectuals with a nationalist agenda, both from the right and left. In addition, there were members of the Arab Socialist Union, easily identifiable in their semi-official outfits, as well as the Security Squad of the Revolutionary Committees, who didn't differ in their dress or appearance from the members of the Arab Socialist Union.

Uthman ended up flying back and forth from Tripoli to Turkey without ever contacting Rahma. Ten long years after their one-night stand, Uthman would find himself face to face with our hero, Mukhtar, without even registering his presence. Instead, oblivious to the park, its inhabitants and history, he went to Adrian Pelt Street, where our heroine insisted they meet. She took him to see the statue in the museum. Whenever they get together during those ten years, she tells him again and again about the magic and the curse of the statue. The statue is her only preoccupation, from the moment she enters his beach house to the moment she leaves, many hours later. One can say that, when she was with Uthman, the statue was her favourite flavour of gum. Like Mukhtar, she too is a victim of the nineteenth-century statue and its curse, which destroys whoever becomes conscious of its neglected presence in the hallway of the museum. The surrender in the statue's face and the forthright willingness of its body is the seed of all this destruction. She wanted Uthman to experience all of that. Instead, he ignored the statue and concentrated on her small body. She felt the heat of his eyes on her skin while she talked to him about the statue. Uthman saw the statue several times in the company of Fatma, and didn't care much for it. It was Fatma who, in his eyes, became the statue. He saw only her and the gum. She was his delicious gum, and he believed that his desire was reciprocated. He jokingly described the nature of their relationship to his friends as a reciprocal chewing: 'I chew her and she chews me.' Life for Uthman was an exercise in this form of unconscious chewing, and he absorbed all the teachings of the prominent Professor of Philosophy, recently returned from France. Maybe this was the secret of his immunity from the curse.

Although they only met once, Rahma and Uthman continued to chew on their first meeting for ten years. Their lives seemed uneventful and free from the preoccupation of chewing. His life was occupied by business, travels and long nights. Rahma's life was taken up by visits, shopping and smoking her hookah. He didn't succumb to the curse of the statue, nor did she experience the curse of the park. She isolated herself in her house and he focused on his business, and they appeared to live like everyone else. Perhaps it was because of their age, or their relationship with Turkey.

—— ✿✿✿✿✿ ——

The Story

The story goes as follows: Mukhtar, the son of a former Royal Police officer, meets Fatma, the daughter of an employee in the Ministry of Religious Affairs. After a brief love affair, she leaves him and he waits for her in the park where they first met. Fatma leaves in search of money and a different life, before turning to prostitution at a time when the country is experiencing the chewing hum craze. Turkey becomes the primary exporter of gum, using carpetbaggers as couriers. This is the story, everything else is peripheral.

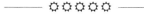

The Statue 2

The statue, standing neglected in one of the hallways of the Red Palace, suddenly acquires a national and cultural value thanks to the interest of a Professor of Archaeology. Completing his studies with distinction, he wrote a book on Libyan sculptures during the Augustan period. He travelled throughout the 'Libyan continent', a term he coined to describe the country, inspecting its cities and archaeological sites. He passed through Akakus, Matkhandush, and took pictures of the prehistoric oases with his camera, which he fondly nicknamed Old Lady. Unlike other Libyan researchers, he climbed Zankakara Mountain to inspect the Garamantes' horse drawn carts. He considered them the most valued treasure of Germa, the pinnacle of Libya's journey towards civilization, which began, according to archaeological finds, in the Stone Age, passing through the invention of wheels and horse-drawn carts, as well as mummification, dating back more than six thousand years.

The Professor of Archaeology discovered the statue during his pursuit of Fatma and momentarily dropped his professional interest in sculpture. She was walking towards him and he thought she was the most beautiful woman he had ever seen, perhaps even his soul-mate. Her red scarf and black coat attracted him, reminding him of how stylishly French girls dressed. He thought she was probably a student at the Arts Academy. 'Miss!' he called out, pursuing her up the steps to the first floor of the museum. She didn't stop walking until he found himself beside her, facing the statue. The way she looked intently at the statue convinced him she was studying sculpting at the Academy. Without waiting to be sure, he asked her, 'Do you study sculpting? I'm a specialist in the history of sculpting.' She turned to him and immediately saw his fascination with her small body. 'No, I merely study how men turn into statues,' she retorted brazenly. She slowed her chewing and raised her chest, placing one hand on her waist. The Professor of Archaeology froze, conscious of his body acquiring the stillness and paralysis of a statue, despite the feelings raging within him.

She left him standing there. His eyes followed her as she moved away, her black hair covering her small shoulders, her red shawl like a river of blood beneath her hair. He stood frozen in front of the statue. The Red Palace was closing its doors, or maybe it just felt like closing time. He shivered and ran down the stairs to the exit. He stood in front of the Red Palace, facing the Green Square. He was not, however, thinking of the contrast between these two colours as he walked out to the Square. He left the world of sculpture and Archaeology behind and entered the crowded, modern world of people, the world of the Green Square. As she disappeared into the square, her features disappeared from his memory. In his mind, they blended completely with those of the statue. And, lest we meander far from our narrative, let us just say that our heroine became, in the eyes of this Professor, something akin to a sacrifice which must, inevitably, perish the moment it leaves the museum and steps onto the street. Our heroine can be safely carried off to the hospital, the morgue and the grave. Like all statues, she dies the moment she leaves the museum. This is the basis of the Professor's particular theory of archaeology: artefacts are to be isolated from the present in order to discern the characteristics of their own age.

Statues such as ours, however, are living artefacts, despite their stillness. Their own histories begin the moment the sculptor picks up his chisel. A spatial relationship evolves, capturing the mood of the people around it. Some visitors develop something akin to love, and find themselves engaged in a playful relationship, while others end up hating them. The statue, abandoned in the Red Palace in the nineteenth century, had survived several Libyan eras, its own existence threatened many times over. As we saw, the identity of the sculptor was something of a mystery, although he was assumed to have been an Italian prisoner. However, the Professor of Archaeology attempted to prove that the sculptor was in fact a Libyan whom the Italians had kept captive for ten years, during which time he had learned his craft and made the statue for an Italian landowner. He was eventually released and repatriated to Tripoli, where he was imprisoned in the Red Palace for the offence of making idols. As an act of rebellion, he created the statue, capturing the contradictory notions of surrender and impulsivity and angering the Turkish governor who ordered him to be executed. The statue was destined to remain overlooked except for the one guard who kept it a secret and meditated daily on the stone woman's beauty.

Our statue is an embodiment of smoothness and violence, stillness and propulsion, pleasure and pain, the angelic and the demonic, the feminine and the masculine, all dryads born in captivity, in the absence of freedom. The few who know the piece are aware of these intrinsic anomalies. The statue came into being as a result of contradictory needs on the part of its sculptor. The darkness of the Red Palace, the rays of light that streamed through the small high window near the roof, the cold, the dampness, the stifling heat and extreme humidity of summer, the overwhelming longing for the female body, the terror of impotence, the signs of divine mercy he longed and waited for, the raging anger at fate, all of these and dozens of other contradictions contributed to the birth of this artefact.

Until the Italians discovered it in Tripoli, the statue waited every morning with pursed lips for rays of light to kiss it warmly. It suffered through long, cold nights and damp winters. It was a vital body, throwing itself headily towards the light, its face surrendering to its warmth. It stood suspended and motionless, eagerly pursuing a mirage of light and warmth. When the Italians moved the statue out of the basement of the Red Palace, its new conditions, sunlight and warmth, improved its mood. Onlookers sensed its gentleness as their eyes feasted on the statue's new found well-being. The statue, like all sculpted forms, was created to be seen, its essence fed by the eyes, the imagination, the feelings of onlookers, and, without these elements, it would remain a lifeless object. The sculptor who created this dazzling form was a sensitive man, to whom the female body became an obsession. The idea of the feminine stimulated his most exalted ecstasies with its beauty and softness, and yet maddened him with his inability to possess it. He began sculpting in order to destroy the arrogance of that image, he had a need to hold it and break its power, and masonry was the only means at his disposal. Working with stone changed his mood as the body began to appear more supple and yielding. His desire for destruction was transmuted to soft, gentle touches. The details of the face and hair and the softness of the form subsumed his other desires. The sculptor longed to disappear in a watery, liquid medium after years of clawing and struggling, but he, of course, never succeeded in conquering his desires until the day he died in the Red Palace's dungeon. During those years, the sculptor lived in a state of levitation, in worlds he had never before experienced, where everything disappeared except the statue that would eventually enter oblivion, sharing the fate of other such artefacts. The sculptor's incarcerated body longed to jump beyond confinement, his own pursed lips longed for a kiss that was never given.

The Professor of Archaeology's studies of Libyan sculpture in the Augustinian period led him to notice many characteristic features. A self-erect sculpture such as ours was, however, not typically Libyan. Roman sculpture in Libya, from the twelfth till the fourteenth century, had been carved into rock. During his travels all over the country in search of the remains of Libyan sculptures – from Aslanta in the Jabal al-Akhdar, to Qarza in the Bani Walid, from Kakus south to Tarhuna north – our Professor of Archaeology found not a single erect carved statue. Never severed from the stone, statues of this period were more like appendages or umbilical cords connected to their source, as if they were newborn babies dragging their womb behind them for their entire life and well beyond death. Autonomy would result in a splintering and, in the process, a destruction of the carved object. The Professor of Archaeology believed that this explained the relationship of the individual to the tribe in Libya. Libyans are attached to their tribes, each dragging it like an umbilical cord behind him.

Coarseness was another of the features exhibited by sculptures from that period of Libyan history, recalling the naïve and hasty traditions of the Phoenicians. The Phoenicians were nomads who rode the camels of the sea. The softness and care attended to our statue went against the argument of its having a Libyan source. The Professor of Archaeology saw two exceptions to these general rules, and both were traced to the fourth century in one of the valleys of Bani Walid. One depicted a Libyan in traditional garb, holding a dictate from Leptis Magna, a Roman settlement, that assigned him the governorship of Ghirza, while the other was of a Libyan woman wearing her national dress with her hair tied up in a kerchief similar to those still worn by the women of central Libya. According to the Professor of Archaeology, these statues, like many of the statues from the Roman period, demonstrated how Roman governors in Libya had mimicked Latin culture and art. But those particular statues remained Libyan in the coarseness of their execution.

The Professor of Archaeology stopped searching for Fatma after that single meeting. He didn't look back, although he often saw her beside the statue. She had led him to the sculpture, but that was all. He was not drawn to her feminine restraint. He was a man who knew his statues and Fatma didn't belong among them. He traced the names of Libyans who had mastered drawing in the European style through their travels to Turkey. Some had studied in Istanbul, which was, at the time, whirling with European influence. The sculptor of our statue was not among them. Most of the artists had stuck to the medium of drawing and none were imprisoned in the Red Palace. The Professor resorted to his European connections to discover whether any Libyan had sculpted anything in Italy during the nineteenth century. He was greatly discouraged when nothing turned up and he became the subject of ridicule to Europeans and Libyans alike. Long neglected in the hallways of the Red Palace, the statue almost destroyed the Professor's career. His theory of the Libyan origin of the statue was far-fetched and lacked scientific basis. His research was seen more as a reflection of his inflated nationalistic sentiments. He left everything – his house, his job, his friends – and stood for long hours gazing at the statue, paying no heed to the remarks of visitors and museum employees, who nicknamed him 'The Second Statue.' The Professor became part of the very room that housed the statue. In time, he was overlooked and forgotten, despite the inconvenience of his presence. Only Fatma knew the Professor's fate.

After months of despair, the Professor of Archaeology had his hopes somewhat raised when he found a statement indicting a man in his forties for apostasy and idol worship. He discovered this evidence in one of the records of the Red Palace, which he had looked over many times before without noting anything of interest. The condemned man had been caught molding human figurines from clay. Statues of women and drawings of naked females were found in his home as well as a representation of the Earth in the shape of a ball. He was summarily executed. With this document, the Professor of Archaeology became more certain than ever that the statue was the creation of this one man. He didn't, however, possess any tangible proof that there was a relationship between them and thus remained unable to publish his findings on the subject.

The Park 2

The neglected park where our hero Mukhtar stood for ten years attracted the attention of several organizations. His presence transformed the park into a theatre, reflecting all the important changes in society. Books, plays, music and articles, not to mention endless academic studies and media programmes, both visual and audio, were produced to analyse various aspects of the park. Amidst all these goings-on, our hero remained on the periphery, almost forgotten. He was the genesis of all this coverage and yet became gradually more incidental in the studies of the Professor of Philosophy. The same can be said for the studies of the Professor of Economics, who incorporated the Professor of Philosophy's ideas into his own teachings. These studies became part of the phenomenon, along with the empty wrappers and the paper on Libyan consumerism, and were included in the one theatrical production put on by the Theatre Director.

As we have pointed out, the park reflected all the changes the country had gone through, but all these ideas were eventually forgotten. Crowded with all types of people, the neglected park become a rubbish heap, its pathways blocked by litter. Even the narratives that drew on the park as a theme were eventually ignored. When asked to be specific regarding the setting of their stories, writers would often mention a place altogether different from that particular park. Thus, the park suffered from neglect despite its role in Libya's modernization. Here, one can cite the nationalization of the Sanitation Company and all the nationalistic prose and poetry composed on its behalf. This, in its turn, gained the interest of an Environmentalist recently returned from the United States after an absence of over twenty years. He was an enthusiastic man, a lover of nature, who, after a catastrophic career as a teacher in America, had come back without a degree. But he found many open doors waiting for him in Libya. Despite his lack of academic qualifications, he managed to convince the authorities to adopt his project. His primary focus was our park. The Environmentalist organized a cleaning campaign, which was manned by volunteers. The Municipality of Tripoli provided them with the necessary equipment, including trucks to remove the rubbish from the city. As a result, the park blossomed. Even the trees looked greener and flowers began to bloom.

These tangible results allowed the Environmentalist's reputation to rise quickly. He became a frequent guest on popular radio programmes, and his activism began to receive attention in the newspapers, giving much needed coverage to the environment and the park. Thus the park blossomed after many years of neglect. A local environmental organization was formed, which included on its board the artist who we previously saw trying to depict our heroine in the European fashion. Also on the board were the Professor of Economics, the Theatre Director and the Professor of Archaeology, many shady businessmen and, no doubt, several security officers disguised as public servants with a casual interest in horticulture.

At their first meeting, the Board members were reserved, being chiefly concerned with their personal agendas. The Professor of Economics emphasized the necessity of cutting down the decorative trees in the park, which, in his opinion, were a symbol of a capitalist system, and substituting them with trees that would bear fruits like apples, pomegranates, oranges and dates. His vision for the park was that of a people's paradise, where children could run and play whilst eating its fresh produce. The park could be subsidized with the money collected from entrance tickets sold for a token amount. Another member of the Board was a security officer disguised as a flower producer, who had successfully amassed a fortune selling flowers for state festivities. He suggested establishing small flower kiosks as a solution to the endemic problem of people uprooting them in the park. He proposed a monetary fine for anyone caught picking flowers. The painter suggested holding exhibitions in an open studio for talented artists, especially children. This suggestion was favourably received. The Professor of Archaeology's suggestion to move the neglected statue from the Red Palace to the park where Libyans could get to know their history and its aesthetic value was the only idea that was rejected outright. The Professor resigned from the Board, declaring that it had no interest in promoting beauty, culture or history. Ultimately, none of the proposals were implemented, except the flower kiosk, set up the day after the meeting, and the fines, imposed on all who illegally picked flowers. Men from The Flower Security Squad apprehended and fined anyone who dared to do so. Yet somehow the park experienced a new lease of life. The sanitation workers began watering the trees and grass again, the park's patrons changed, and the only constant was our hero, standing in the rain.

As we have mentioned, the history of the park paralleled Libya's history. It was constantly threatened with annihilation and yet it endured. It remained a verdant, flowery place, sometimes frequented by lovers, amateur poets, penniless strangers looking for sanctuary and by prostitutes who chewed their gum and ensnared their customers. Formerly adjacent to Adrian Pelt Street, the park now found itself next to Municipality Street. Thanks to the efforts of the Environmentalist as well as to happy coincidence, Libyan families began to go there in summer, in search of a clean, safe escape from the suffocating heat of their homes. Throughout its long history, from the time when the Turkish governor had forced its peasant owners to sell it so that he could turn it into his own private estate, the park had had very few Libyan visitors. It was a place denied to Libyans, except perhaps several lone outcasts: dancers and drummers, hustlers and con men in Sufi guise, and a few popular poets selling their fawning verses. The park had always been, in media speak, a 'den of iniquity', where Libyans barely spent more than a day. The exception was one singer who sang there for ten long years. I have no idea why the figure ten seems to crop up as often as it does.

The singer, whose voice enchanted all who heard it, came from Fezzan, in the south. She carried the rhythms and melodies of Fezzan to Tripoli, and sang to console herself now that she was in a new city far from her family and loved ones, whom she had left behind in order to escape poverty and hunger. The park was the only place in Tripoli the singer knew. She suffered from the humidity, the cold and the terrifying crash of waves. Every night, her songs filled the park, drowning the sounds of the sea. Every night, until daybreak, the songs of Fezzan bathed Tripoli and its park in tears, longing, pain and despair. All those who heard the woman from Fezzan sing knew her only by her soft, sad voice. The Pasha had ordered that she should sing from behind a curtain, which gave her a semi-mythical stature. This anonymity allowed all who heard her to imagine her in any form they liked. Thus she was, by turns, dark-skinned, olive-skinned or black, tall or short, slim, or, as most desired, plump.

On her way to Tripoli, the singer from Fezzan had looked like an ordinary woman in the eyes of her travelling companions. She was one of seven women on the caravan and probably drew the least attention. Unlike the other women, she was the only one who was not a slave on her way to be sold in the markets of Tripoli. She was a free woman from a family ravaged by poverty. Some of her tribe had chosen to remain in the oasis, battling hunger, while others, like her, had travelled north or south. When she arrived in Murzuq, the singer broke into song, realizing how far she had travelled. The sound of her soul's longing and sorrow made the caravan suddenly stop. Her voice was like a winged creature that transported the men and women in the caravan to their own, distant desires. The singer's voice was distinguished by its ability to capture the longing of all who heard it. The Bedouins were transported to their watering holes, the sons of oases to their origins, and, more importantly, lovers to the arms of their beloved.

Zubayda from Fezzan arrived in Tripoli as a migrant,

to earn a crust, as the saying goes, and, two days after her arrival, she became a slave who sang of longing and painful desire, without anyone seeing her. One of the merchants on the caravan was so enchanted with her as she sang from behind the red robe that he advised the Pasha to have her always sing from behind a curtain, adding to her mystery. The curtain certainly gave the lady from Fezzan many forms of beauty, and caused much argument and fighting among the Pasha's park visitors. Tales of love affairs and secret meetings circulated, when in truth the only man Zubayda knew was the Pasha. One of those lovers was another singer from Tripoli, who had been smitten by Zubayda's voice. He wanted to see her and listen to her songs in person. The Pasha refused, considering it a privilege merely to sit gazing at the curtain while she, on the other side, sang alone. Despite the curtain, the singer from Tripoli had better luck than many other admirers. He had talked with her, listened to her and got to know her. Even with the curtain, he could roughly guess her shape, while she engaged him with talk about the singing of Fezzan or Tripoli, regaling him with songs no one else in Tripoli had ever heard. He reciprocated with his own songs, and together they formed a duet on warm Tripoli nights.

The Pasha watched what was transpiring between Zubayda and the singer from Tripoli. It was certainly unusual on his part to let things develop the way they were and the moment came when both singers felt safe enough to hold hands. At that instant, daggers appeared from nowhere, cutting down the male singer. He dropped dead before Zubayda's eyes, dragging down the curtain with his body. Zubayda didn't scream or utter a single word. Instead, she remained resolutely silent until her eventual solitary death in the park. No one ever knew that the mute who haunted the gates of the park was Zubayda, the singer from Fezzan, whose voice had enchanted all of Tripoli and whose songs were sung by the women of the city whenever they felt claustrophobic and in need of soaring away. The park, with its trees and birds, its Pashas, and its slaves and honoured guests, had come to love the voice of Zubayda, and yet, in the end, her corpse was left out for the dogs. However, neither the dogs nor the Pasha could erase the timeless longing that Zubayda had had for the oasis, the dunes and the palm trees. That longing can still be heard today, many generations later, by those who know nothing of the singer.

Many other women's wretched fates became intertwined with the park. Some committed suicide by hanging themselves from its trees, while others were buried in unmarked graves. Despite its opulence, the park became a prison and a cemetery for women. The second Pasha, who inherited the park from his father, was so disturbed by its history of orgies and decadence that he came up with a cruel scheme that saw the park transform into a strange laboratory producing black babies with blue eyes and tiny noses, blondes with kinky hair, big lips, full breasts, wide hips and long legs, and black women with long limbs and small breasts. The second Pasha supervised these experiments himself, pairing blonde women with black men and black women with blonde men. The couples lived together for four months, then were separated as soon as the woman became pregnant.

Women who didn't immediately become pregnant would be circulated among the men until they conceived. The experiment went on day and night.

The first Pasha had been killed by a Turkish Officer. That officer's wife, Lilla Nasima, used to come to the park from time to time and was a favourite of the Pasha. At her arrival, he would leave his other guests and attend to her. She was Turkish, but the strong sun of Tripoli had tanned her fair skin and the Pasha fell in love with her. His infatuation was no secret to any of the park's regulars, as the Pasha would get drunk and chase her openly. When he caught her, he would tear off her clothes and take her on the grass. Their laughter, panting and screams could be heard across the park. No one could object, or express disapproval about what took place between the Pasha and Lilla Nasima. No one came to the rescue that ill-starred night as Lilla Nasima escaped whilst her husband slaughtered the Pasha. The guards killed the Officer when they saw him chasing his naked wife, and then discovered the naked Pasha slain on the grass, wearing nothing but his tarboosh. Lilla Nasima fled naked from the park and disappeared from sight for six years. She was found dead in the fourth year of the Italian occupation. The details of her life during those years of disappearance are unknown. She didn't leave Tripoli as some have claimed. According to one account, Lilla Nasima lived not far from the park, outside the gates of Tripoli in a small house owned by a fisherman. He discovered her naked the night of the incident and decided she must be the jinn he had long been expecting. Ever since he had learned to fish with his father, he had dreamed of a jinn emerging from the sea, who would bring him happiness and wealth. Although this one had appeared rather late in life, he was still glad she had come at all. These were his thoughts as he saw her standing alone and naked. He had never imagined the jinn would be naked, or that he would find her curled up like a child bereft of its mother.

In disbelief, he sat in front of her for long hours. All her inconsolable weeping and obvious misery couldn't convince him she was human, let alone that she was Lilla Nasima. He gave her the room where he slept and took to sleeping in the adjoining room. He would hear her weeping all night. Without exchanging words, for that was not possible with her endless weeping, he realized, after many attempts, that it was futile to encourage her to speak or eat. She remained in that condition for four days, then told him during her first meal that her name was Nasima. He asked her if she was Lilla Nasima, and, laughing bitterly, she returned to her silence and food. After several months, she convinced him to go to her house and learn the fate of her only daughter, who had been left in the care of the maid. He didn't go to the house but tried to discover the news from afar. He learnt that the maid was still employed and getting ready to marry a merchant from the south. Lilla Nasima followed her daughter's news without ever seeing her again, even from a distance. She took comfort in the fact that the maid had not abandoned her after the marriage.

The fisherman married Lilla Nasima, who lived in complete isolation. Her husband and the house were all she needed until the Italian artillery bombarded Tripoli, destroyed the house and killed her husband. She emerged from beneath the debris with a deep gash on the side of her head. In a daze, she found herself wandering in the park at night and hiding in the ruins of her house in daytime. It was during the fourth year of occupation that she was found dead. Before her death, Lilla Nasima wandered the park at night, rambling about the fisherman, her daughter, her murdered husband and the slaughtered Pasha, whom she kept seeing running naked in the park with his tarboosh.

Violent confrontations between the Libyans and the Italians watered the flowers with blood. The park remained too desolate for people to enter, resembling an abandoned bride in all her finery and overpowering perfume. People began to think of it as a haunted place. The ghosts were those of Libyans and Italians, the screams were of raped women, and of those who had killed themselves, the moaning was of the wounded, the smell was of the dead and tortured. The earth was ploughed over, and the park's flowers and grass pulled up, although its trees were left in place. Workers came with their camels, donkeys, and ploughs to lay the foundation for an Italian park on the ruins of the Turkish Pasha's pleasure park. The new layout seemed like a new beginning, a celebration, a discarding of mourning clothes. Once the Italians decimated the Resistance, Tripoli became an Italian city. During this era, the park finally became what a true park should be. New workers and new visitors began coming. They were mostly Italians, for the park was designed primarily for them and only a few Libyans were allowed in.

——— ✧✧✧✧✧ ———

The Father 2

As we have pointed out, Omar Effendi was not a native of Tripoli. Like other Bedouins and farmers, he arrived in search of work and, like many of them, he immediately joined the Police Force set up by the British. This Police Force was inherited by the Monarchy after Independence. Omar Effendi didn't consider himself a British heirloom, but a son of the Kingdom and one of its faithful guardians, who had not abandoned faith in the institution despite its political collapse. Following his release from prison, Omar Effendi retired and settled on a farm that produced chickens, eggs and milk. Deserting his family, he became infatuated with the younger generation of prostitutes. He had not seen his wife in ten years and asked his son not to come to the farm. He sent both of them money with one of his labourers at the beginning of every month. Omar Effendi had become infatuated with our heroine. It was love at first sight and, of course, he was entirely unaware of her relationship with his son.

It was as if he had found everything he was looking for when he first laid eyes on her. Our heroine Fatma was the model of this new stage in Omar Effendi's life. Her jet-black hair, short stature, black eyes, and small breasts, were the epitome of youth and health. Sitting next to her on their first meeting, he experienced a rush of warmth running through his veins. There was no need to kiss her or sleep with her; all he wanted was to be close, to draw the warmth out of her, the delicious waves that lapped leisurely at every cell in his body, making him feel as though he had just woken from a long sleep.

He had known many women, but had never experienced such simple pleasure, which involved neither dance, nor drink, nor nudity. Fatma filled that space and provided that lightness. He began to withdraw, to abandon his usual pastimes. He became satiated. He would sit quietly in front of her as though he were reclining beneath the sun on a cold winter day, soaking in its rays. When she left for a few minutes, his body would contract as if it were conserving its energy.

He succeeded in conquering his coughing fits, his heart rate grew steady and he experienced serenity. He ceased talking in her presence, for talking became the slayer of emotions. He rediscovered the sensation of grass that he had long been afraid to touch or look at after those calamitous shootings long ago. He started to wake up early every morning and walk barefoot on the grass. His soul picked up the sound of his bare feet. He would sit on top of a hill on the eastern edge of the farm, waiting for daybreak, and then stretch out on the wet grass, exhaling the memory of the sounds the bodies had made as the police shot them down. He would weep at the memories. Chickens, baby chicks, and even pigeons, would strut across his body as it lay prostrate on the grass. Some would peck his face. In this peaceful submission, Omar Effendi began experiencing the last stages of his life through Fatma. Fatma came regularly to the farm and would sit in front of Omar Effendi without saying a word or even looking at him, still as a statue. She realized that, regardless of whether it was through the father or the son, she was, in fact, undergoing the same experience. The statue was still chasing her and it was set on destroying everything. The father, like his son, had acquired a statue-like silence which she had sought to escape when she had left Mukhtar standing in the park.

Omar Effendi came to the realization that every age has its own pleasures. His long life had given him opportunities to experience everything. Fatma was slowly teaching him how limited those pleasures had been. Success in life had meant attaining all a person could want, but, Omar Effendi had always seen the end of each day as a defeat. Now he realised that man's journey, however bright and promising, is always the road towards that sunset. Dancing, food, wine and girls had been desperate attempts to pin down one true moment of existence, and he had failed each and every time. Now he was living the sunset of his life in calmness and solitude, submitting to the moment without struggling to hold onto it. Fatma coaxed him to the beauty of a quiet ending he could never have imagined. He was filled with happiness, released from his obsessions.

After their first meeting she had disappeared for a few days and he had keenly felt her absence. Omar Effendi was used to being dismissive and not caring about anyone. He had only ever been focused on the woman standing before him at that exact moment. He sought only the tremors and the signs of pleasure that his fingers released in their young bodies. There was never much variation, nor did it matter who the woman was. Fatma was unlike the others. He experienced pleasure simply by being in her presence. A hot wave washed through his veins as though her breaths were gusts of hot wind. And, unlike the others, the pleasure of her presence lingered after she left. The warmth remained. At their first meeting, he had felt awkward and inept. It had been a new experience for him. He had not been expecting anyone and her small frame, her audacity and her erect nipples had taken him unawares. There she was – a rare blend of forwardness, lust, childhood, innocence and reticence. This blend was her secret and Omar Effendi had inadvertently stumbled upon it. He tried to convince himself she was simply a newfangled type of prostitute when, in fact, she was probably the least skilled of the lot. She was neither beautiful nor playful, and so inexperienced that he looked at her in pity as she took off her black coat and approached him. She looked like a beggar, extending her innocent lips in a request for alms, or a granddaughter asking her doting grandfather for money to buy some gum. As it happens, Fatma really was looking for money to buy gum, not for the sake of gum itself, but in that it was a steppingstone to a new future. Omar Effendi knew nothing about gum, or the value it had for Fatma and society at large. After her quick exit, he requested Ghouiliya to pay special attention to her, because – although he believed all women to be artificial adornments whose shine only lasted a few years –he felt that this time he had found, in his words, a 'true jewel.' When she left the farm that day, Fatma forgot all about Omar Effendi. Enthusiastic about her new commercial venture, she got down to the business of chewing and scouting customers. She wanted her autonomy, to build a house, to find a husband and achieve security. Omar Effendi was a customer, an excellent and distinguished one at that, but nothing more.

In that first week after her encounter with Omar Effendi, she met a Building Contractor in a café by the marina. He sat down beside her without asking permission, ordered his coffee and asked if she was waiting for someone. His audacity threw her off guard, but she soon discovered this was how they all behaved, in a pragmatic manner that didn't waste time. If a girl was asked if she was waiting for someone and responded in the negative, then that was taken as an implicit consent that they could spend the night together. The Building Contractor kept her at his farm in Wadi al-Rabi' for three days. He took her virginity for the price of a thousand dollars. Despite the pain, she saw it as a good deal. Exhausted, she returned to Omar Effendi who ordered dinner and let her sleep. He sat beside her for a long time before lying down gently next to her as his pores absorbed the warmth of her body, just like the hero in The House of Sleeping Beauties by the Japanese Nobel-laureate Yasunari Kawabata. At dawn, he rose quietly so as not to disturb her and tiptoed out into the garden, leaving the door to the room and the house open behind him. His white jilbab was barely visible in the silver white of dawn and he sat enjoying the cold dew on his skin. With sunrise, his goose pimples disappeared and he lay on the earth as birds gathered around him. Fatma, meanwhile, was stretched out on the bed, releasing the exhaustions of the previous night while dreaming of lying upon soft grass with a green horizon extending into the blueness of the sky.

When he returned to his room, Omar Effendi didn't have much to say to Fatma. He found her awake, staring into space. He sat facing her like the night before, marveling at the amazing juxtaposition of innocence, lust, impulsivity, submission, audacity and boldness that she displayed, in the same manner as a cat flexes its claws. Seated on the bed, she told him she had slept deeply. He didn't answer. She said she was tired from the previous nights, but that she was feeling better. She then stood up on the bed, looking like a statue of alabaster in her white jilbab. He remained, grave-faced, in his chair. She placed her right foot on his left shoulder, while he gripped her left leg with one hand and lifted the other to her as if in supplication. He didn't want anything. It was as if he was admiring a stone statue rising from his bed. After a few moments, Omar Effendi felt his strength wane and the heat of her jilbab suffocating. He got up with difficulty and his right hand reached out to hold her breast under the jilbab. On touching her skin, he gasped and fell to the floor. A few minutes later, he was dead. Thus, Omar Effendi passed away, just like that, in the style of a melodramatic folktale. All it took was one line. Fatma remained standing over him like a statue in her white jilbab, her mouth gaping. People received the news of Omar Effendi's death quietly, even coldly. Some expressed surprise he was still alive. His wife didn't care and asked the farm workers to take care of the funeral arrangements. She found a lawyer to handle all legal matters related to the estate. His son, our hero, remained standing under the tree in the park, waiting for our heroine to turn and run back to him.

Fatma didn't leave the farm. She remained there for days. Ghouiliya told her the life story of Omar Effendi: the unusual details of his past in the Royal Police Force; his relationship to the park; his obsession with the memory of the dead bodies of students falling onto the grass; and their revolt against the King and the foreign bases. Our heroine was familiar with most of the details from his son Mukhtar.

Rahma

What truly amazed Fatma was what Ghouiliya told her about Rahma, Omar Effendi's wife and Mukhtar's mother. For the past ten years, Rahma had lived alone in her house on Ben Ashur Street, smoking her Turkish hookah. Fatma had not known that the mother of our hero had a connection to Turks and hookahs. According to Ghouiliya, Rahma was of Turkish blood on her mother's side. Her grandmother died at the beginning of the Italian occupation of Tripoli, leaving her daughter to be raised by a Libyan family who married her to their only son. Rahma was the result of that union. Her father died in the Second World War fighting in eastern Libya and she was raised by her grandmother, who arranged for her to be married to Omar Effendi after Independence. Thus Rahma was 'cut off from the tree,' as Ghouiliya put it, in reference to her being orphaned and then living alone for years after being abandoned by Omar Effendi the moment he was released from prison. Despite knowing these details, Ghouiliya had never met Rahma or even seen her.

Armed with this information, Fatma realised that Mukhtar was the key to the success of her project. He was rich and had no siblings or cousins on either his father's or his mother's side. Therefore, she could make him hers and become everything to him. She left the farm and went to visit Rahma. Fatma waited for a few moments after knocking on Rahma's door and was not allowed in until she told her that she knew Mukhtar and wanted to see her. Rahma was not as excited as Fatma had expected. When Fatma walked into the living room, she said she was a friend of her son's, that she saw him every day and that he wanted to marry her. 'Congratulations!' Rahma replied, smiling sarcastically. She sat on her chair next to the hookah, offering Fatma a seat as well. Fatma continued talking about Mukhtar, their mutual infatuation and their intention to marry and settle on the farm. She asked her to join them so they could take better care of her. Rahma remained silent for a moment, staring at her before simply replying: 'You're a liar!'

Fatma couldn't believe her ears and Rahma repeated herself. The girl realized she was in the presence of a stubborn Turk, but decided to hold tightly to her project in the face of Rahma's cold reception and condescending gaze. She visited Rahma's home frequently from then on, attempting to soften the stubborn mother without once returning to the subject of Mukhtar, who remained waiting in the rain.

Rahma soon realised the young lady really did have her son under her spell and would be difficult to ignore. It was then that she decided to get to know her. Rahma, who chewed on her single night with Uthman, saw from her second encounter with Fatma that she was also a constant chewer and that this habit must involve her only son Mukhtar. Rahma now became part of the chewing aficionados. It was only after the death of her husband that Rahma remembered her long forgotten son. Fatma was the one who had reminded her of him and she realised that this new girl was the inevitable future from which she couldn't escape. What Rahma didn't know was that Fatma, the way into the future, also had ties to her past, to her husband and his death. Fatma had emerged from her past to give birth to her future. This sort of pretentious philosophising about the history of Rahma and her son takes us back to the Professor of Philosophy, who is currently living the leftist phase of his fiery article, Existence: Gum. This shift from right to left happened suddenly, like all momentous events. The Professor of Philosophy woke up one morning, the day that Omar Effendi died, let us say, opened the window overlooking the garden of his small house and saw flowers blooming, despite the fact he had given up on them the previous evening. Without bathing or washing his face, he sat down to write an article inspired by the event, entitled 'Hope'. His first line was a variation on the maxim of Mao Zedong, 'Let one hundred flowers bloom.'

The Professor of Philosophy completed one intellectual phase and entered another with a single stroke of his pen. He began his piece with Mao Zedong, the legendary enemy of flies, as a way of apologising for his previous devotion to Sartre and his flies. He had postponed this shift for rather a long time, waiting for the right moment. During this leftist phase, the Professor met Rahma. They were in a new department store under the management of some capitalists who had been given permits to import a few items, which included, among those most notable to our story, gum and plastic roses, which Rahma particularly loved. Rahma was a regular customer who had bought many types of flowers in order to create a 'garden' in a corner of her house. The Professor of Philosophy was attracted to blooming roses but felt only disdain for the crowds queuing for gum in the candy section. This was when he saw Rahma, a blooming rose from a beautiful past that had been nurtured under the right temperature and climate. He knew that the roses were not real. In his philosophical optimism, however, they represented a way of creating beauty out of ugliness, of having flowers bloom from oil.

On the day she met the Professor of Philosophy, Rahma's perfume overpowered the plastic odours of the store. She noticed the Professor with his suit and necktie. It was a long time since she had seen a man so elegantly dressed. The Professor of Philosophy was attracted to her perfume and the way she blushed. Like any elegant Parisian, he selected a flower from one of the baskets and happily prepared to pay for it in order to offer it to the beautiful woman before him. The seller, however, shocked him by declaring the store didn't sell single flowers but only bunches of five, at six dinars each. Dividing the money for each flower became a complicated procedure and when that was accomplished the Professor discovered he didn't have any small change. Coins were almost never used, despite their virtual existence on price tags. Without more philosophising, the Professor of Philosophy pulled six dinars from his pocket and took a single flower. He made his way towards Rahma, and, with a Parisian bow, offered the token which she accepted, bringing it up to her nose and whispering demurely, 'Merci.' The Professor of Philosophy, who had dedicated himself to mapping the changes of human life, felt his whole life turn upside down. He was now looking at the glass half full, while ignoring the empty half. Staring at

Rahma, he spoke the words that he, his students and fans would consider to embody the next important phase of human change. He said, 'Life is a glass half full.'

At that moment, the Professor of Philosophy was filled with a new outlook on life, so very different to the one he had previously held. He who had experienced poverty at a young age, and who had borne the burden of philosophy for so long, was always drawn to pain for the sake of philosophy. Standing amid the artificial flowers, Rahma offered him the simple joy of life. In her eyes, his well-tailored suit and necktie were tokens of elegance and order in a chaotic world. The Professor of Philosophy thus embarked on a wholly new phase, proffering a plastic flower as he approached Rahma. She represented a historical moment, as though she were an island in a turbulent sea where he had been battling with the cruel and painful destiny of man. The artificial flower garden in the small, crowded department store with its overpowering plasticky odours suddenly became a Garden of Eden, manufactured by humanity despite its wretched existence and inevitable destiny. All because of Rahma's presence.

Rahma dragged the Professor of Philosophy by his necktie to the left of Sartre. She didn't know who Sartre was and didn't care about human destiny, or even philosophy. She was a woman who had lost everything: husband, son and lover. She had no companions except her hookah. She didn't know she was Turkish or that she had been abandoned and betrayed. She had probably always thought of herself as the betrayer who abandoned and deceived everyone and everything. In those first moments, Rahma felt an unusual shyness as she listened to the Professor of Philosophy express his extreme admiration for her beauty and elegance. She had not known there were men with such high standards in the country. All she knew were those who pulled their trousers down after one word of hello. This even included Uthman and it was at that moment she realized he would never come back. The pleasant and elegant lover in front of her would be her final destination. She went out to a café with him and drank Arabic coffee. She smoked the hookah as he watched her in disbelief, a true companion whom he would never let escape. He asked her to marry him and she accepted without a moment's hesitation.

Despite his 'intense dislike of communism' the Professor of Philosophy saw in Comrade Rahma, as he called her, a true partner in a society where such qualities as she possessed were few and far between. She drank wine, smoked the hookah and discussed sex, religion and Arabs as if she were the true granddaughter of Kemal Ataturk, despite being illiterate and not even knowing who Mr. Kemal was. She was a secularist by nature. She was the Simone de Beauvoir of the Third World, a liberated widow with a Professor of Philosophy the equal of Sartre. Libya can be a surprising country! They didn't discuss the details of their marriage, and certainly not the dowry. All they knew was that they were an unusual couple in an unusual time and place and that, after drinking coffee and flirting with one other, they would head for their marital nest to make love as two lovers should, without any need for a religious ceremony.

They would remain comrades to the end, according to the law of choice.

As Rahma moved to the next phase of her life with the Professor of Philosophy, she forgot everything: her son, her dead husband, Fatma and ¬– ultimately – her project of marrying off her son and thereby ridding herself of the farm. Life began for her at that moment. She stared into the Professor's eyes without noticing his unusual form of myopia. He was handsome, and even more elegant than he had first appeared now that he had become her companion. 'Life begins now!' was the phrase that she kept repeating to herself as she inhaled her hookah and gazed upon him. At that moment, Fatma knocked on Rahma's door. No one answered. Fatma continued to knock, confident that Rahma would be alone and would, undoubtedly, open the door.

7

The Hero 2

Time is the enemy of one's first love. The war between time and love erupted at creation and seems likely to continue until the end. Love tries to stop the flow of time while the flood of time seeks to break down the fragile dams of love, held up, above all, by art. Mukhtar, our hero, spent the first years of his life not knowing what true love was. Like everyone else, he went along with the flow of time, bending to its rhythm as it dragged him towards expected endings. He jumped from his mother's lap into the street and school, learning, like all others, what he was taught, and dreaming conventional dreams. He never experienced anything different, nor did he seek to achieve anything out of the ordinary. He loved many women and many fell for him, with the usual conclusions. He was a prisoner of time. He never felt a need to fight it. Time moved towards a future where he saw only the beginning of life and not its end.

The moment Fatma left him, he became aware of a more terrifying aspect of time – the human push towards an end, towards oblivion. Love was suddenly dragged off and strangled with her red shawl. Pieces of it went flying everywhere behind her. She was walking in step with time, while he struggled beneath the rain, trying to hold on to the last moments of her presence. Those moments, as her figure grew smaller, were his personal doomsday. He struggled in the rain for ten long years to postpone the inevitable, to rewind everything to the beginning and remain there, at that moment, as though he could thereby triumph over time. He stood there, just like the statue that had brought them together. Like any abandoned lover, he entered a dark night, a mirage, while he ran towards her, standing motionless as she moved away. The abandoned statue in one of the hallways of the Red Palace had shown him all the contradictions of impulsivity and immobility, exactly as gum had shown her surrender, recklessness and haste. The moment she walked away in the rain, shrouded in her black coat and red shawl, he began to churn those moments, holding on to her and the flow of time that dragged him further into the darkness and the unknown.

Standing in the rain for ten long years was our hero's reality. Like a mythical god, he had thrown his magical staff into the wheels of time to force them to a halt, just a few millimeters before they crushed his love beneath them. He didn't defeat time. She continued to walk away, her red shawl swaying from her small shoulders as she set off towards the sunset. He had stopped time, but he couldn't turn back the clock. She continued walking. Our hero was truly living a life of stasis, far from all the pretentious philosophising with which most writers pad the empty lives of their heroes, thereby permitting themselves the privilege of speaking on their behalf and exercising control over human fate, albeit the fate of imaginary fictional heroes. Our hero remained as still as a statue, defying the terrifying flood of time as she walked away. She had escaped. She was a few metres away, her hair swaying on her shoulders and her red scarf hanging loosely against her back. The blackness of her coat erased her from his sight. Nothing new can be added to the fate of our hero after that. All that ensues is the churning and chewing in which our narrative is eternally trapped. Despite all the structural and stylistic tricks we have employed to extricate ourselves from this novelistic nightmare, we remain in a state of endless chewing.

But then again... What if we were to try another game? What if we were to stutter? Stuttering is a form of word-chewing or to be precise, a form of letter-chewing. Stuttering suits our hero and is a particularly human act. But who is stuttering? Is it our hero, or is it time? Mukhtar's stuttering is normal. He stuttered as a child and his mother took him to see several doctors, all of whom failed to cure him. After many years and many visits to private clinics, she finally became convinced that stuttering was simply her son's fate. Stuttering, which many suffer from, is not a purely Libyan phenomenon. However, it acquired its scientific dimension in the country with the return of a Professor of Psychology from Germany, where he had obtained his PhD in psychoanalysis, having studied the works of Freud and Jung. He had become obsessed with Freud in the seventies when he was still in high school. Life soon became a large mirror reflecting everything Freud said and everyone became a Freudian creature. He discovered that the stutter his father suffered from was nothing more than the struggle between the id and the super-ego, with the id screaming and the super-ego squashing him underfoot.

Stuttering is the escape route that we propose for our text. We have, without realizing, already laid the groundwork through our reference to the novel of the late Egyptian writer Ihsan Abdel Qaddus, The Well of Deprivation, in which the writer focused his creative efforts on applying the theories of Freud to his characters – or rather, creating characters to fit his Freudian theories. Therefore, there is no harm in speculating on the theory of stuttering and returning to the Professor of Psychology, who saw the world through a Freudian lens. Upon his arrival in Libya, he pursued his interest in stuttering, giving it a collective dimension through the theories of Jung. According to the Professor of Psychology, stuttering was a social byproduct rather than an individual condition. The connection between this and our hero is not immediately apparent. However, one day the Professor of Psychology read an article about him for, as we have said, our hero had become the subject of countless newspaper articles. After reading these accounts, the Professor of Psychology could barely conceal his excitement as he prepared to examine our hero. He headed straight for the park and stood for some moments, observing him as he struggled through the night mirage, beneath the tree. Our hero was waiting for her to stop, turn and run back to him.

Initially, the Professor didn't see a relation between our hero and stuttering, but after hearing him utter a few obscure words, he froze and cried out 'Eureka!' as all great discoverers do. He pulled a notebook from his pocket, which he carried with him wherever he went so as to jot down any observations, regardless of their apparent importance, a habit he had learned from the Germans. He wrote three words: 'He really stutters.' By being motionless, our hero was forcing time to stutter, just as he stuttered in his speech. Thus he gained the attention of another of the experts recently returned from overseas. His immobility in the park gained new Freudian and Jungian dimensions. Looking for live samples is a major difficulty in Libya, especially in psychology. Despite the many human specimens available, there are always numerous impediments standing in the way of any true research. Our hero offered a rare opportunity for Libyans recently returned from Europe and America. Mukhtar represented a freely available sample for a wealth of different arenas: philosophy; psychology; economics; theatre; television; media. Furthermore, he was a specimen with negative implications and, until then, all negative phenomena had been discussed only in general, abstract terms. One would refer to reactionary forces, opportunists, the sick and many other types without specifying any one person in particular. While stuttering gives our text a chance for continuity and progress, it also marks the beginning of the breakdown of its fragile structure. It represents an attempt to escape from the position of 'stasis', to chip away at the statue, and gain a victory, albeit a small one, for gum. Standing still is a mute act while chewing is a stuttering one.

The Professor of Psychology stood beside our hero, encouraging him to speak and overcome the shyness caused by his stuttering. He kept repeating that stuttering was not shameful, but the result of social repression, beginning with the family and extending to the street and the school where he had been victimised. At that moment, our hero felt a strong and sudden desire to move beyond his motionlessness and reach for gum. Chewing, with its upward and downward motion, had abandoned him beneath the tree. He stuttered her name and thus revealed the secret he had hidden in his immobility for ten long years. Through the guidance of the Professor of Psychology, he stopped chasing the mirage. Our hero left the park. He didn't think of his mother, his father or his house. She was the only creature that he tried to hold onto after his escape from the night mirage. She was his target as he crossed streets that had changed much since last he had seen them, when she had left and he had stayed behind.

She was not in the museum, and certainly not in the park. Nor could he see her under the Dakheliyyah Arches where he used to wait for her, taking shelter from the burning sun and sudden downpours of Tripoli, thanks to the sagacious planning of its Italian architect. She was sitting in a coffeehouse, packed with foreign women and Libyan men. She was alone. He approached her. She didn't notice him. He brought his lips close to her ear in order to whisper a few words when a strange smell overpowered him. It was a feminine smell, but it was not her smell. She jumped up and looked at him with eyes that were wholly changed. The make-up, despite its thickness, couldn't conceal her exhaustion and pain. Her short stature, which had always attracted him, now repulsed him with its added weight. He realized that for ten years he had stood motionless while the flood of time had defeated him after all. Thinking he was a customer, she invited him to take a seat before reeling off the conditions for the night ahead. He jumped up and moved away, stuttering curses totally incomprehensible to her. He headed for the museum, certain that the woman he had met in the café couldn't be Fatma, who would instead be waiting for him beside the statue. He entered the museum in a hurry and walked straight to the statue where the Professor of Archaeology remained. He rushed to embrace the statue, flinging his arms around it so violently that it fell to the floor and shattered into pieces. He continued to curse incomprehensibly. He left the museum, not knowing where to go. The Dakheliyyah Arches that used to protect him from the scorching Tripoli sun couldn't protect him from his internal fires. He was alone, exhausted, a stranger walking purposelessly up and down the street. No one paid him any attention. His feet stumbled for days along the street without anyone giving him a second glance: not Fatma, not his mother, not all the Professors of Economics, Philosophy, Archaeology and Psychology; not even the journalists and radio show presenters. He had become a memory that might perhaps be mentioned in a brief footnote. Our hero had entered a long, long night, alone, exhausted and emaciated.

Chewing gum piled up on shelves as a result of an economic open door policy. Shops were packed with shampoo, bananas, and magazines. The country had turned a page. Our hero was no longer motionless and chewing gum had triumphed.

Retrato del autor: © JOANOT CORTÈS

Agustín Bernaldo Palatchi

Agustín Bernaldo Palatchi, nacido en Barcelona en 1967, es jurista. Dedicó cinco años a investigar en profundidad una época histórica fascinante, sobre la que siempre quiso escribir, y el resultado fue *La alianza del converso*, publicada por **Roca**editorial. *El gran engaño* es su segunda novela, en la que trata temas que, por su experiencia profesional, conoce de primera mano.